This book belongs to:

_____

_____

Dedicated to the Harvard Square chess hustlers who still mystify me.

- P.A.

To my siblings - playing board games, we shared life's lessons in victory and defeat.

- O.C.

To my family, thanks for your love and support.

- J.C.

immedium
inspiring a world of imagination

Immedium, Inc.
P.O. Box 31846
San Francisco, CA 94131
www.immedium.com

LIBERUM

www.liberumdonum.com

First hardcover edition published 2023.

Edited by Don Menn
Book design by Monika Mandreza

Printed in China
10 9 8 7 6 5 4 3 2 1

Library of Congress Cataloging-in-Publication Data

Names: Amara, Phil, author. | Chin, Oliver Clyde, 1969- author. | Calle, Juan, 1977- illustrator.

Title: The discovery of chess : the Asian hall of fame / by Phil Amara & Oliver Chin; illustrated by Juan Calle.

Description: First hardcover edition. | San Francisco : Immedium, Inc., 2023. | Audience: Ages 5-12 | Audience: Grades 2-3 |
Summary: "Dao, a red panda, guides Ethan and Emma, two school children, back into time to discover how chess was created and became popular worldwide"-- Provided by publisher.

Identifiers: LCCN 2022052811 (print) | LCCN 2022052812 (ebook) | ISBN 9781597021623 (hardcover)| ISBN 9781597021630 (ebook)
Subjects: LCSH: Chess--History--Juvenile literature.
Classification: LCC GV1446 .A44 2023 (print) | LCC GV1446 (ebook) | DDC 794.1--dc23/eng/20221116

LC record available at https://lccn.loc.gov/2022052811

LC ebook record available at https://lccn.loc.gov/2022052812

ISBN: 978-1-59702-162-3

The Discovery of
CHESS

The Asian Hall of Fame

शतरंज की खोज

immedium

Immedium, Inc.
San Francisco, CA

by Phil Amara & Oliver Chin
Illustrated by Juan Calle

At the park, Emma and Ethan saw a crowd gathering around some tables.

"What's going on?" asked Ethan.

"Let's see," replied Emma. Pairs of people played the same game, staring at small figures on a square board.

One player quietly moved a white piece and stopped her clock. It was her opponent's turn.

His clock started, and he decided where to move a black piece. A kind voice whispered, "Do you want to learn more about chess?"

It was Dao You! This friendly red panda had shown them fantastic inventions that came from Asia. "Sure!" they answered.

ASIA

INDIA

POOF!

"Then buckle up," laughed Dao. "This battle of wits has entertained people for centuries."

"People have always played games," Dao continued.
"Most historians think chess started in one place."

Dao took out his special gong.
When hitting it with his mallet,
he transported them to a distant
place and time. Gooone!

Whoosh! From a puff of smoke, the trio emerged in a faraway land. "Where are we?" asked Emma.

"This is India in 500 C.E.!" announced Dao.

"Watch out!" cried Ethan as a parade of fearsome elephants stomped by.

WHOOSH!

India was split into dozens of kingdoms from north to south. "Each fought for supremacy," explained Dao.

VS.

But perhaps a *raja* could use "war" games instead. A leader could practice pitting his warriors against a foe.

An ancient Indian army was composed of *chaturanga* (Sanskrit for "four arms").

The first was infantry,
rows of low-ranking
foot soldiers.

PADATI

The second was cavalry.
Mounted on horses or camels,
they charged with lances.

ASHVA

The third were chariots. Pulled by horses, these heavy wooden carts carried commanders and archers.

RATHA

The fourth were elephants. They were trained as prized "shock" troops that could break through an enemy's lines.

GAJA

Chaturanga became a game's name. On an *ashtapada* (an 8x8 board), four players each controlled 8 pieces (raja, cavalry, chariot, elephant, plus 4 infantry), which had different moves. The goal was to capture the other kings.

Dice were used for gambling. For two players, the sides were red versus green. The number of troops doubled. Strategy changed. The raja paired with a *vizier*, a wise advisor. "It was battle without bloodshed," inferred Emma.

Zip! In the 6th century, the trio followed traders west on the Silk Road to Persia.
Now called *chatrang*, the game of chance became one of skill.
Dao said, "Chariot in Persian was *rukh*."

Ethan said, "The chariot became the rook!"

Whizz! In 700 C.E., Arabs conquered Persia. In Arabic, chatrang became *shatranj*. King was *shah*. "A winning player said *shah mat*," Dao noted. "That meant 'the king is frozen.'"

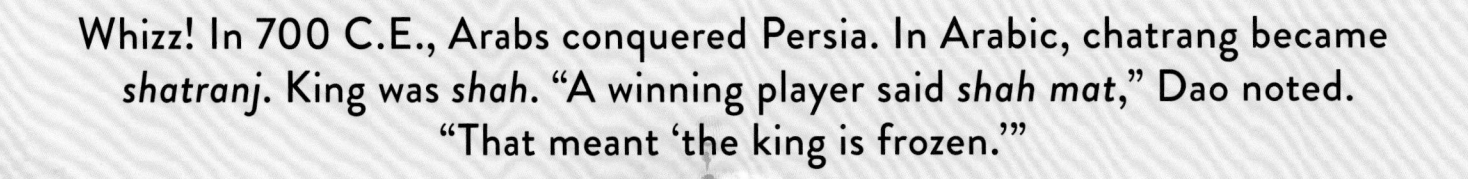

DOME OF
THE ROCK

Emma said, "*Shah mat* became 'checkmate'!"

Zoom! In the 8th century, from North Africa, the Moors seized Spain. In Europe chess joined checkers and backgammon.

EUROPE

SPAIN

GREAT MOSQUE OF CÓRDOBA

"The board got checkered," Emma observed.

"The pieces became black and white," noted Ethan.

The elephant became the far-reaching bishop, reflecting the Christian church's influence. "Chess was a pastime for royalty," remarked Dao.

"Sets were carved from deer antlers, and elephant and walrus tusks," said Emma.

The cavalry became a knight on a horse. "A 12th century book said a knight needed seven skills," Dao reported. "One was being good at chess."

ISABELLA

Then in the Middle Ages, the weak vizier was replaced by a strong queen.

"The first female, she became the most valuable piece," stated Dao.
"The queen was the power behind the throne."

In the 17th century Enlightenment, passion for chess spread to everyone.

"Thank the printing press,"
said Ethan.

KLINK

CLANK

EMPRESS
MARIA
THERESA

MORALS
– OF –
CHESS

Zap! In 1771, in the Austrian court
the Mechanical Turk became known as a
miraculous machine that defeated humans!

"Meanwhile in the American colonies, chess gained
fans such as Benjamin Franklin," declared Dao.

Later, after touring continents, the Turk was uncovered as a fraud. "Across the world, some tried to ban chess, citing its bad influence," sighed Emma.

"But chess has inspired even more artists and authors," asserted Ethan.

In 1851, Howard Staunton hosted an international tournament in London.
Opening with the King's Gambit, Adolf Anderssen won the "Immortal Game."
In 1857, the US had its first championship. "Skill brought fame," said Dao

In 1886, the US hosted the first world championship.

"Cuba's José Raúl Capablanca won his first title in 1921," said Ethan.

"A Russian refugee, Czech Vera Menchik was the first women's champion in 1927," announced Emma.

Vera is the only woman who plays as a man.

Zing! After helping crack Germany's secret codes in World War II, Alan Turing invented a chess computer program in 1950. But former allies, the USA and Soviet Union waged a "cold war." Chess became a battleground.

The Soviets dominated world championships from 1948 to 1972. At 14, Bobby Fischer won his first of eight US titles. Then in 1972, the 29-year-old whiz toppled champ Boris Spassky to be America's first world chess king.

In 1974, computer programs dueled in their own contest.
"Nona Gaprindashvili was from the Soviet republic of Georgia," said Dao.

"She became a woman's champ and then the first female grandmaster in 1978," said Ethan.

In 1975, Russia's Anatoly Karpov succeeded a reclusive Fisher. In 1983, the novel *The Queen's Gambit* featured a girl prodigy. The next year, Karpov and Azerbaijan's Garry Kasparov played 48 games in 5 months, then had to restart!

"Kasparov prepared for a rematch. Blindfolded, he faced 10 players simultaneously," said Dao. "He conquered 32 computers in 5 hours. Then at 22, he became the youngest champ and then the #1 player for more than 20 years."

КАРПОВ

КАСПАРОВ

In 1989, Kasparov trounced IBM's supercomputer "Deep Thought." But in 1997, an improved "Deep Blue" program (calculating 200 million moves per second and 40 moves ahead) finally beat him in 6 games.

I will defend the human race.

GARRY'S 1999 RECORD 2851 RATING

DEEP BLUE

Behind the iron curtain in Hungary, the homeschooled Polgar sisters became grandmasters. “At 15, Judit earned the rank faster than Fischer,” said Emma. “She was the #1 woman for 26 years and highest ranked female ever.”

"In 2000, Viswanathan Anand won the first of five world titles," said Dao. "Anand became India's greatest player."

"At 16, Hikaru Nakamura won the first of five US titles in 2005," said Ethan. "He specialized in speed."

THE LIGHTNING KID

TEHRAN, IRAN 2000

Chess.com

THE SPEED DEMON

At 13, Norway's Magnus Carlsen became a grandmaster. Kasparov advised him. In 2013 he dethroned Anand. Studying computer matches, he scored the highest rating ever. In 2021, he won an 8 hour game of 136 moves.

2021
5x champ

CHENNAI, INDIA

2882
RATING IN 2014

IN 2022, I SOLD MY COMPANY PLAY MAGNUS GROUP FOR $83 MILLION

Passion for chess endures in popular culture through television, movies, politics, and business. More kids than ever play around the globe. "That reminds me," cried Dao. "It's time to go home." Dao hit his gong. Gooone!

Whoop! From a magic cloud, they returned to the park.

Some read to learn patterns from historic games.

Others jousted with adversaries or computers online.

Practice required concentration, confidence, and creativity.

Emma said, "I want to join the local chess group."

Ethan said, "I want to start a school club." They waved goodbye to their dear guide.

Dao shouted, "On the board and against the clock, have fun and be good sports!

GLOSSARY

Arabia
Founded by Muhammad, the religion Islam spread from the Arabian peninsula. Its empire (632 C.E.-1258) spread chess.

Ashtapada
Chaturanga's 8x8 board. Four players each had 8 pieces and used dice. Later two players each had 16 pieces.

Bishop
Each moves diagonally, but only on the square's color that it starts on. An intimidating Indian elephant became an influential Christian priest.

Chaturanga
An ancient Indian board game considered chess' precursor. The Sanskrit word of an army's "four arms" or divisions: infantry, cavalry, chariot, and elephant.

Checkmate
Chess' goal is to attack the opposing king. If you place him in "check," and he cannot legally move to escape, then you win!

Enlightenment
Europe's "Age of Reason" (late 17th century - 1815). Printed paper spread knowledge. Scientific, political, and philosophical ideas drove social change.

Grandmaster
In 1950, 27 players were awarded this highest rank. Now 1,700+ players (1,300+ active) are "GM," a title held for life.

King
Moving one square, the most important piece in chess is the only that cannot be captured. Protect yours. Try to "check" your opponent's.

Knight
The only piece that jumps over another. It moves in an "L" shape from one colored square to the opposite. Thundering Indian cavalry became a leaping horse.

Middle Ages
European period from the Roman Empire's fall (5th century C.E.) to the Renaissance (15th century). Catholicism shaped the continent's culture.

Moors
Moroccans or Muslims of Spain and Portugal. They founded the Islamic Andalusian civilization (711 C.E.-1031) and resettled in North Africa.

Opening
A player's first several moves of the game. Strategy comes from hundreds of classic sequences. The middlegame and endgame follow.

Pawn
The weakest piece in chess. But if one of 8 foot soldiers crosses to the other side, it is promoted into a stronger piece (but not a king).

Persia
Stretching from Egypt to Pakistan, this empire (559 - 331 B.C.E.) was a hub of trade and cultural exchange.

Piece
A pawn, knight, bishop, rook, queen, or king. Each moves in different ways and directions.

Queen
The only female on the board is the strongest piece. By the king's side she commands all the moves except the knight's.

Raja
An ancient Indian monarch. This chief ruled the army's four divisions. In chaturanga, he became the king.

Rook
The second strongest piece moves horizontally or vertically. An Indian war chariot became a castle's tower.

Sanskrit
The ancient classical language of India and Hinduism. Historically written in Devanāgarī and other scripts.

Shah
A Persian sovereign. In Arabic, *shah mat* means "the king is frozen." That phrase became "checkmate."

Speed
This game format has fast time-controls. The main types are rapid (10+ minutes/player), blitz (3-5 minutes), and bullet (3 minutes or less).

USSR
Union of Soviet Socialist Republics. Formed after World War II, when Russia expanded its territory. Made of 15 republics, the nation dissolved in 1991.

Vizier
A king's chief minister. In chaturanga, he moved one square diagonally. In Europe, the powerful queen replaced this weak counselor.